In My Momma's Kitchen

In My Momma's Kitchen

Jerdine Nolen

illustrated by Colin Bootman

SCHOLASTIC INC.

New York Toronto London Auckland Sydney
Mexico City New Delhi Hong Kong

ISBN 0-439-28317-5

Text copyright © 1999 by Jerdine Nolen.
Illustrations copyright © 1999 by Colin Bootman.
All rights reserved.
Published by Scholastic Inc., 555 Broadway, New York, NY 10012,
by arrangement with Lothrop, Lee & Shepard Books,
a division of William Morrow and Company, Inc.
SCHOLASTIC and associated logos are trademarks
and/or registered trademarks of Scholastic Inc.

12 11 10 9 8 7 6 5 4 3 2 1   1 2 3 4 5 6/0

Printed in the U.S.A.   14

First Scholastic printing, February 2001

Oil paints were used for the full-color illustrations.
The text type is 18-point Novarese.

First in Line

Seems like everything good that happens in my house happens in my momma's kitchen. Like the day Nadene burst in waving a letter over her head.

"I got it!" she yelled. "I got it!"

"What?" I shouted back. "What did you get?"

Nadene held the letter over her heart and closed her eyes. She read the whole thing without even looking at it:

> "Dear Miss Jefferies:
>
> I am pleased to inform you that you have been accepted to our university on a four-year music scholarship. . . ."

We did a dance around Nadene. Momma and Daddy hugged each other real tight. Then Nadene got out her clarinet and played Daddy's favorite song, "This Little Light of Mine." Daddy sang a made-up song about Nadene being the first person in our family to go to college:

> "This little daughter of mine,
> First in the family line.
> This little daughter of mine,
> She's made it to college time.
> This little daughter of mine,
> First to be in line,
> Going to college,
> Going to college,
> See her shine!"

I felt so proud, I stood on a chair and saluted her.

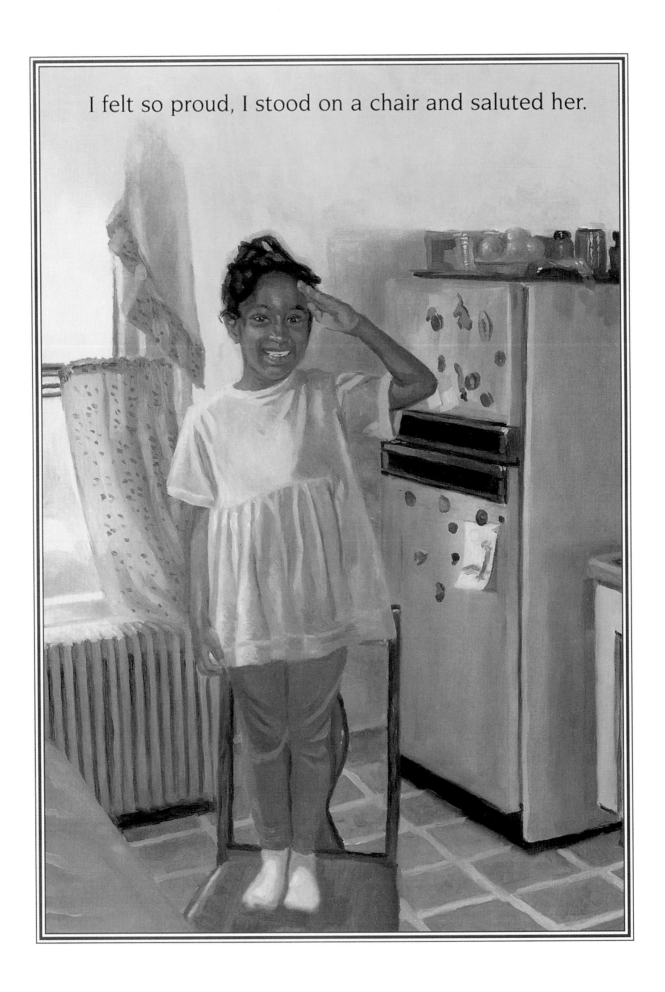

The Wedding

My friend Naomi made all the plans. We held Emma's wedding in the sunniest part of Momma's kitchen, right under the window. We marched her down the aisle between Momma's African violets.

Janie was supposed to be the groom, but she squirmed and meowed and wiggled out of her wedding clothes.

Then she hid behind the stove. We had the reception anyway: tea cakes and ice-cold buttermilk. The groom came back when she saw the buttermilk.

Talking Pots

On the Saturday Momma and her sisters do Talking Pots Day, I stay close by. Aunt Katie, Aunt Gloria, and Aunt Ludie always arrive together. Each one is carrying her biggest stewing pot in one arm and shopping bags in the other.

The bags Aunt Ludie carries are full of vegetables.

Aunt Gloria's bags are filled with meats and sausages and always one odd-shaped package on the top. We all know what's inside it: the biggest soup bone in town.

Aunt Katie's bags hold extra cutting boards, knives, vegetable peelers, bowls, and spoons. She pulls them out. Then she holds up Gran Lee's metal coffeepot. "I'll make the coffee."

In moments every hand is busy. Nadene and Momma are washing vegetables when Momma begins to hum a melody that has no words. Then Aunt Ludie joins her in deep low tones. Aunt Katie and Aunt Gloria chime in with high-pitched harmony. The air is full of humming. Their hands are flying. I think they cook like hummingbirds.

Just as easy as the music started, it turns to talk.

"Remember the time you told me the insides of the human body smelled like fresh pineapple?" Aunt Ludie asks as carrot peelings fly into her bag. "I got laughed right out of seventh-grade science class that day!"

"Remember how Momma always bragged about the way I chop onions?" says Aunt Gloria as her knife *ca-chunks* on the cutting board. "Always minced so nice and fine and never a tear!" She sighs, shaking her head.

"How 'bout that time you made my Easter dress on the sewing machine, Nell?" Aunt Katie, seeding tomatoes, says to Momma. "Not one of you had the heart to tell me the hem was four inches longer in back than it was in front. I couldn't figure out why Reverend Taylor looked at me so funny when he shook my hand."

All day the kitchen is busy and full and cozy. Even the African violets are blooming, just like my aunts.

Great-aunt Caroline

When Great-aunt Caroline came to spend her ninety-fifth birthday with us, Daddy was glad. I wasn't.

"Why do we always have to be so quiet around Great-aunt Caroline?" I asked Momma.

"She's very old," Momma said. That didn't seem like a very good reason to me.

Great-aunt Caroline wasn't used to cats, so Janie had to sleep in the basement. Great-aunt Caroline wasn't used to children underfoot, so Naomi couldn't come over. And Great-aunt Caroline always sat in *my* chair and called it *her* chair.

She was still sitting there while I cleared the table one morning. Henry, her walking stick, rested on her lap. I figured she was watching to make sure I did a good job, but by the time I had finished, her eyes were closed. She sat completely still. It didn't look like she was even breathing. Had she died? I held my own breath as I leaned over to look in her face.

Suddenly she opened one eye, just like Janie. "Boo!" she shouted. "Gotcha! I made you look. Ha-ha-HA-HA-HAAAA!"

Later, when we went for a walk, she called me her "Walking Out to the Backyard Friend."

Janie's Apples

Every October, Momma makes crab-apple jelly. I wash the apples, Nadene peels them, Momma cooks them, and we all fill the jars. It gets pretty busy, so usually Janie hides behind the stove. Usually—but not this time.

This time she marched into the middle of the kitchen and jumped on top of a basket of apples. Momma shooed her, but she wouldn't get down. I put her on the floor, but she jumped right back up and rolled around.

"Shoo, Janie," I scolded. She batted an apple, then another and another. I think she thought the apples were mice. Just as I reached down to pick her up again, she batted one mouse too many. The basket fell over, and the apples came crashing down around her.

Apples rolled all over the floor. I tripped and fell right on top of Janie. Janie howled. Momma dropped a pot of water. Nadene screamed and grabbed for the mop.

By then Janie was frantic. She ran around the kitchen, but she kept running into apple baskets. She knocked every single one over. Then she slid through the puddle of water and crashed into the wall.

Just then, we heard Daddy at the door. Janie scrambled to her feet, let out a wild "Meee-oooow," and flew outside right between his legs. He stared after her. Then he stared at the mess in the kitchen. Finally he looked at the three of us. "Cat got everyone's tongue?" he asked. And we all burst out laughing.

Corn-Pudding Time

Most of the time, we say the kitchen is Momma's. But when Daddy makes corn pudding, it belongs just to him.

At the first crackle of the falling leaves, he announces, "It's getting to be corn-pudding time!"

As soon as the first frost covers the ground, he rubs his hands together and sniffs the air. "Mmmmmmm," he says. "I can almost smell that corn pudding cooking up right now!"

By the time the pumpkins have all become sagging jack-o'-lanterns and pumpkin pies, Daddy has taken over the kitchen.

Watching Daddy make the corn pudding is a lot better than actually eating it. While he turns the handle of Momma's old-fashioned eggbeater, he sings "La Cucaracha" and dances the cha-cha.

While he sifts and stirs, measures and mixes, pours and pinches, he sings and dances the tango right across the kitchen floor.

"Mmmmmmm," he says as he slides the corn pudding into the oven. "This is going to be the best one yet!"

Then he picks me up, and we twirl and swirl around the room.

Corn pudding has never been a favorite dessert of mine. But when Daddy presents it at the dinner table wearing that smile of his and humming "Glory Hallelujah," having to eat it is worth it.

Winter and the Gran Lee

In winter when I come home from school, the warm kitchen fogs the windows. I hug Momma from behind, and she says, "Hello, Sweet Potato Pie. How was school today?" Then she drops a taste of peach cobbler into my mouth, and peach juice dribbles down my chin.

"Stand close to Gran Lee and warm the shivers off," she tells me. Then we talk about my day while she stirs a pot of greens, turns the frying chicken, and mixes a bowl of corn-bread batter.

Chum, chum, chum, chum, Momma's wooden spoon scrapes against the bowl. But before she can put the corn bread into the oven, she jiggles and shakes the door handle.

"I don't think I'll remind Daddy that the handle is still broken," she says to me.

I smile. Gran Lee was Momma's momma's stove, and she doesn't want a new one. Neither do I.

Nighttime Serenades

Sometimes in the middle of the night I wake up. When the house is dark and quiet, I can count the ticks of the clock. Four hundred ninety-three . . . four hundred ninety-four . . .

I go into the kitchen for something to eat. Sometimes Daddy and Janie are already there. We sit and snack together on whatever we like. Sometimes we make sandwiches out of leftovers and have ice cream and cookies. We giggle and munch and try not to wake the others. We talk in whispers and make big gestures, but Daddy isn't all that good at being quiet.

Clang, bang, a lid falls on the floor. Soon Momma and Nadene are in the kitchen too, and Daddy doesn't have to whisper anymore.

"Now that we're all here, how about a story?" Daddy asks. Then he starts the way he always starts: "When I was a little boy down on the farm . . ."

After the story come songs. Daddy calls them "Serenades for Sleepless Nights."

We sit around the table talking and singing and laughing just like that's what everybody does in the middle of the night.

And when I finally start to yawn, I know for sure that everything good that happens in my house happens in my momma's kitchen.